Soccer Crazy

by
Gilles Tibo

illustrations by
Bruno St-Aubin

Scholastic Canada Ltd.
New York Toronto London Auckland Sydney
Mexico City New Delhi Hong Kong Buenos Aires

Scholastic Canada Ltd.
604 King Street West, Toronto, Ontario M5V 1E1, Canada

Scholastic Inc.
557 Broadway, New York, NY 10012, USA

Scholastic Australia Pty Limited
PO Box 579, Gosford, NSW 2250, Australia

Scholastic New Zealand Limited
Private Bag 94407, Botany, Manukau 2163, New Zealand

Scholastic Children's Books
Euston House, 24 Eversholt Street, London NW1 1DB, UK

Library and Archives Canada Cataloguing in Publication

Tibo, Gilles, 1951-
[Nicolas, fou de soccer. English]

Soccer crazy / Gilles Tibo ;
illustrations by Bruno St-Aubin ;
translation by Petra Johannson.
Translation of: Nicolas, fou de soccer.
ISBN 978-1-4431-1371-7
I. St-Aubin, Bruno II. Johannson, Petra III. Title IV. Title:
Nicolas, fou de soccer. English.

PS8589.I26N4913 2012   jC843'.54   C2011-905998-3

6 5 4 3 2 1   Printed in Canada 119   12 13 14 15 16

To the beautiful Zia
and her mother, Eveline
— *G. T.*

To Manuel
— *B. St-A.*

Nicholas was nervous. In a few hours, he and his friends were going to play in their first soccer tournament!

He had no time to lose. He needed to practise. He threw his soccer ball against the wall and tried to catch it with his feet. BANG! BAM! BOING!

His mother opened his bedroom door and said, "Nicholas, your soccer is getting on my nerves!"

"Sorry, Mom. I won't do it again."

Nicholas stopped throwing his ball against the wall. Instead, he practised his aim by tossing his ball at the ceiling. But suddenly, CLING! His ball crashed into his reading lamp. BANG! It fell to the floor.

His mother came into his room again. "Nicholas, your soccer is getting even more on my nerves!"

"Sorry, Mom. I won't do it again."

Nicholas put his lamp back. While bouncing his ball off his elbows, his knees and his feet, Nicholas finally managed to get dressed. But when he tried to put on his shoes, BADABANG! Nicholas fell down.

Nicholas's mother opened his bedroom door.
"Nicholas, your soccer is really getting on my nerves!"

"Sorry, Mom. From now on, I'll be as good as gold."

Nicholas dribbled his ball into the kitchen. He dribbled by his mother, who was reading the paper. He dribbled by his father, who was having a coffee. He barely got by his sister, who was just sitting there!

But suddenly, while trying to dribble past the cat, Nicholas messed up. The ball bounced against the fridge, and SPLAT! It knocked over his sister's cereal bowl.

"Nicholas, your soccer is getting on EVERYONE'S nerves!" said his sister.

Nicholas tossed his ball into the living room, but SPLASH! It landed right in the aquarium.

Nicholas's dad picked up the ball.

"Nicholas," he said. "Your soccer is getting on my nerves!"

Nicholas dropped to his knees and begged.
"No . . . please! Don't take my ball away.
Please! I neeeeeed the ball for the tournament!"

13

His father tossed it into the backyard.

"I do not want to see that thing in the house again. Understood?"

"Yes, Dad!"

Nicholas gobbled up his breakfast and went outside. All his teammates met up with him in the backyard. They practised dribbling; they practised their fakes; they practised their passes.

Suddenly, the ball flew over the fence and hit the neighbour's clothesline. All the clothes fell to the ground.

Mr. Hunter stormed out of his house. Picking up shirts and socks, he grumbled: "Nicholas, your soccer is really getting on my nerves."

He scooped up the ball. He looked as though he wanted to squash it!

Rodrigo saved the day . . . and the ball!
"It's my fault, sir!" he explained. Rodrigo
looked up at Mr. Hunter with big, sad
puppy eyes.

Mr. Hunter sighed and said, "Listen carefully. The next time anything happens, the ball disappears!"

"Yes, sir! Yes, sir! Yes, sir! Yes, SIR!"

Nicholas and his team began practising their shots, their fakes and their dribbling again. All of a sudden, after a dizzying scrimmage, the ball shot out toward the kitchen window.

"NOOOOOOOOOOOOOOOOOOOOOOOO!" they all cried.

BOINK!

CRACK!
The window shattered into a million pieces.

Nicholas's dad stormed out of the house and snatched the ball up.

"This soccer is really, really, really, really getting on my nerves!"

Just as Nicholas's dad was about to head back into the house with the ball, little Luigi started to cry.

"*Sniff* . . . we need the ball . . . *sniff* . . . to play in the tournament at the park . . . *sniff* . . . in ten minutes!"

Nicholas's dad grumbled and threw the ball back.
All the kids cheered. "Hurraaaaay!"

Nicholas turned to his father and asked: "Um . . . would you come to the park with us please, Dad?"

Nicholas's father followed the kids to the park, grumbling all the way: "That soccer is really, really, really, really getting on my nerves . . ."

Nicholas's father sat under a tree, still muttering to himself. The referee blew his whistle and the game began! Nicholas and his team used all the tricks and strategies they'd been working on at home.

They dribbled the ball. They made amazing passes, fakes and shots. But the other team played hard too. By the end of the first half, the game was tied 1 – 1. Nicholas was exhausted and hadn't even scored a goal yet.

With two minutes left in the game, the score
was 2 – 2. All the spectators were on their feet.
Even Nicholas's dad!

Suddenly the ball rolled by Nicholas.
He kicked it. The ball sailed through
the air and between the goal posts.
Nicholas had scored the winning goal!

Thrilled, Nicholas and his team walked home. As they walked, Nicholas's dad put his hand on his shoulder and said, "Nicholas, have I already told you . . ."

"Uhh . . . what?"

"I just love soccer!"